Rabbids Invasion

Case File #5: Rabbids Get Access

by David Lewman

illustrated by Shane L. Johnson

Simon Spotlight

New York   London   Toronto   Sydney   New Delhi

This book is a work of fiction. Any references to historical events, real people, or real places are used fictitiously. Other names, characters, places, and events are products of the author's imagination, and any resemblance to actual events or places or persons, living or dead, is entirely coincidental.

Based on the TV series Rabbids® Invasion as seen on Nickelodeon™

SIMON SPOTLIGHT
An imprint of Simon & Schuster Children's Publishing Division
1230 Avenue of the Americas, New York, New York 10020
This Simon Spotlight paperback edition June 2015
© 2015 Ubisoft Entertainment. All rights reserved. Rabbids, Ubisoft, and the Ubisoft logo are trademarks of Ubisoft Entertainment in the U.S. and/or other countries. All rights reserved, including the right of reproduction in whole or in part in any form. SIMON SPOTLIGHT and colophon are registered trademarks of Simon & Schuster, Inc. For information about special discounts for bulk purchases, please contact Simon & Schuster Special Sales at 1-866-506-1949 or business@simonandschuster.com.
Designed by Nicholas Sciacca
Manufactured in the United States of America 0515 OFF
10 9 8 7 6 5 4 3 2 1
ISBN 978-1-4814-3549-9 (hc)
ISBN 978-1-4814-3548-2 (pbk)
ISBN 978-1-4814-3550-5 (eBook)

CHAPTER 1:
Hands Off My Mustache!

One partly cloudy day a boy named Bradley was playing in his yard. Technically it was his parents' yard, since they owned the property, but Bradley thought of it as his.

Even though he was outside, Bradley wasn't playing with a ball or a bat or a boomerang or any kind of toy that was made for playing outdoors. Bradley was playing with a package of fake mustaches.

When his mother had said, "Bradley, go outside and play!" Bradley had grabbed the fake mustaches that were a birthday present from his uncle. He hadn't been too excited about receiving a package of fake mustaches, but he figured today he'd give them a shot.

He picked a mustache, peeled off the adhesive tape on the back, and stuck the mustache on his upper lip. It felt weird. He wondered what he looked like, but unfortunately there were no mirrors in the yard. He tried looking at himself in a puddle, but the mustache fell off and landed in the dirty water.

Bradley peeled the adhesive back off a big gray mustache, stuck it on his upper lip, and pretended to be his grandfather. "I'm grouchy!" he grumbled. "I want to take a nap!" It was a pretty good imitation, except that his grandfather didn't have a mustache. He peeled it off and tried another mustache.

Bradley thought no one was watching him. But he was wrong.

Spying on Bradley from behind a tree were three Rabbids, those mysterious invaders from who knows where! They thought the fake mustaches were some of the most interesting things they'd ever seen.

"Bradley!" his mother called. "Lunch!"

"Coming!" Bradley answered. He was hungry from trying on mustaches. Actually, that's not true. Bradley was always hungry.

He grabbed his package of fake mustaches and ran inside.

But he left one of the mustaches he'd tried on outside. A thick black mustache. The biggest, bushiest fake mustache in the package. (Not the one that fell in the puddle. That one didn't even look like a mustache anymore.)

The second the back door closed, the Rabbids ran toward the black mustache, racing to see which one of them would get to try it on first. One Rabbid was clearly in the lead, but just before he reached the mustache, the Rabbid in second place dove forward and grabbed the prized mustache. "BWAH HA!" he cried triumphantly.

The Rabbid stuck the mustache on his head

4

like a tiny toupee. He struck a pose as if to say, "See how important I look with this tiny toupee on my head!"

The other two Rabbids pointed and laughed. "BWAH HA HA HA!" The first Rabbid scowled.

One of the laughing Rabbids grabbed the mustache and yanked it off the first Rabbid's head. "Bwouch!" the first Rabbid yelled.

The Rabbid with the sticky mustache decided to put it over his eyes like a single long black eyebrow. It made him look mad. "Bwah bwah bwah bwah bwah bwah!" he shouted, pounding his fist into his palm as if he were an angry leader or boss giving a speech.

But the other two Rabbids just pointed at him and laughed. "BWAH HA HA HA!"

The third Rabbid ripped the mustache off the second Rabbid's forehead. "BWOUCH!"

The Rabbid thought for a moment about what to do with the mustache. Then he stuck it on his butt like a tiny black tail. He wiggled his butt proudly.

The other two Rabbids were impressed.

But inside the house, Bradley's mother was *not* impressed. She was annoyed when she looked out the window and saw three Rabbids in her yard. She grabbed her phone and called the Secret Government Agency for the Investigation of Intruders—Rabbid Division (or SGAII-RD for not-very-short).

"There are three of them!" she shrieked into her phone. "And they're in my yard RIGHT NOW!"

CHAPTER 2:

Glyker in Charge

At the Secret Government Agency for the Investigation of Intruders-Rabbid Division, Director Stern had called Agent Glyker into his office. The director was not happy about what he had to say.

"Listen up, Glyker," Stern growled. "I'm going on vacation—a very badly needed vacation. These Rabbids are driving me nuts."

"That's nice," Agent Glyker said. "Where are you going?"

"NEVER MIND WHERE I'M GOING!" Stern bellowed. "That's not important!" He sighed heavily and tried to calm himself. His nephew (Agent Glyker) seemed to have a talent for getting him worked up. "What *is* important is that I'm leaving you in charge."

"Me?" Glyker asked, his eyes getting wide.

"Yes, you!" Stern replied. "That's what I said, isn't it?"

Agent Glyker couldn't help beaming with pride. "It'll be a great honor, sir. I'll make you proud."

Director Stern picked up his briefcase. "Yes, well, I doubt that very much. I'm only leaving you in charge because you'll be the only one here. Everyone else is on vacation or sick or they quit because they couldn't take one more day of chasing these crazy Rabbids."

This didn't discourage Agent Glyker one bit. He was so excited about being left in charge that he dared to suggest, "Then you'd better leave me the key card to the Closet of Super-Secret Experimental Spy Gadgets."

Glyker'd been longing to get his hands on that key for months. He had a key to the Closet of Super-Secret Spy Gadgets, but he'd never been allowed to even peek inside the Closet of Super-Secret *Experimental* Spy Gadgets.

Director Stern hesitated. On the one hand, there were a lot of dangerous, untested gadgets in that closet. On the other hand, he really wanted to start his vacation, and for better or worse, he was leaving Glyker in charge. So he handed Glyker the key card. "Fine," he grumbled. "But while I'm gone, YOU'D BETTER NOT MESS UP!"

He left his office without even saying good-bye.

The second Director Stern was gone, Agent Glyker ran around his uncle's big desk, sat in his comfortable chair, leaned back, and put his feet up. It felt good to be in charge. And he could hardly wait to get his hands on those Super-Secret Experimental Spy Gadgets.

BRRRRING! Stern's desk phone rang, startling Glyker so much that he fell backward onto the floor. *WHOMP!*

He scrambled to his feet and answered the call. "Agent Glyker, Temporary Director-in-Charge," he said proudly. He heard a woman reporting (screaming, really) that there were Rabbids in her yard. *Perfect!* thought Glyker as he hung up. "While Uncle Jim is on vacation, I'll catch these Rabbid intruders all by myself! He'll be so proud of me!"

15

CHAPTER 3:

Follow That Mustache!

When Bradley heard his mom screaming into the phone, he stopped eating his lunch long enough to figure out what she was so upset about: Rabbids in their yard! He ran to the window and stared at the three intruders outside.

"Hey!" he shouted. "They've got one of my mustaches!"

The truth was that Bradley had already lost all interest in the fake mustaches, but when he saw someone else playing with *his* fake mustaches, he wanted them back *immediately*!

Before his mom could stop him, Bradley ran out the door to get his mustache back.

One of the Rabbids had stuck the black mustache on his tongue. He was sticking his tongue out and waggling the mustache up and down. The other two Rabbids thought this was hilarious.

"HEY!" Bradley screeched. "GIMME BACK MY MUSTACHE!"

Bradley ran straight toward the Rabbid with the mustache on his tongue. When the boy had almost reached him, the Rabbid leaped right over Bradley. The Rabbid pulled the mustache off his tongue and stuck it on his stomach.

Bradley whipped around and screamed, "I SAID, GIMME BACK MY MUSTACHE! IT'S MY FAVORITE!"

The three Rabbids looked at each other. The one with the mustache started acting like Bradley, screaming, "BWAH BWAH BWAH BWAH BWAH BWAH!"

He wiggled his stomach, and the mustache fell off, but nobody noticed.

That's when Agent Glyker arrived. On the drive over, he'd decided to not try anything fancy. The second he saw the Rabbids, he'd run right at them and grab one of them.

So that's what he tried to do . . . emphasis on *tried*.

Glyker screeched to a stop, jumped out of his car, and ran into the yard, waving his badge and shouting, "Halt in the name of the SGAII-RD!"

Bradley didn't know what the SGAII-RD was, but he figured anyone flashing a badge could be in charge of recovering stolen mustaches. He ran straight toward Agent Glyker, yelling, "THEY TOOK MY FAVORITE MUSTACHE!"

WHAM! Glyker and Bradley slammed into each other. Bradley went flying over Glyker almost as neatly as the Rabbid had leaped over him. They both ended up sprawled in the grass.

21

"Sorry," Glyker said, helping Bradley up. "Are you okay?"

"I guess so," Bradley said, rubbing his butt. He looked around. "Where did those Rabbids go? They took my favorite mustache!"

Agent Glyker looked around too. The Rabbids were nowhere to be seen. They must have run away when Glyker crashed into Bradley.

Glyker sighed. "I don't know where they went. But I'm going to find them."

Bradley shrugged, not really caring what Glyker did. He ran inside to see if there was any dessert.

Glyker trudged back to his car, disappointed that the Rabbids had run off. By now, he figured, they were probably blocks away in any one of several directions.

But the Rabbids were actually close by. From their hiding place in Bradley's old tree house, they watched Glyker walking away. One of them pointed and whispered, "Bwah bwah bwah!"

On the back of Glyker's beat-up old coat, they saw the black mustache!

Quickly and silently, they slipped out of the tree house and followed Glyker. . . .

23

CHAPTER 4:
Bwhat Was That Noise?

Even though Agent Glyker was discouraged about failing to capture the Rabbids, he immediately felt better when he got back to the office.

He was in charge!

He thought about going back to Director Stern's office and sitting in his big, comfortable chair again. But then he felt the key card in his pocket.

The key card to the Closet of Super-Secret

Experimental Spy Gadgets! The closet he'd been dying to look in!

He practically ran down the hall to the closet. He took the key card out of his pocket and shoved it into the slot under the sign reading CLOSET OF SUPER-SECRET EXPERIMENTAL SPY GADGETS. AUTHORIZED PERSONNEL ONLY!

The automatic door slid open.

Agent Glyker stared at all the wonderful gadgets in the closet. Some were made of gleaming metal. Others of hard plastic. Some looked so unusual that Glyker had no idea what they were made out of.

So . . . which one should he try first?

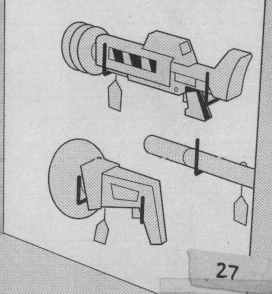

As he was trying to decide, he heard a noise. A familiar noise. A noise that sounded very much like "bwah."

"*Bwah?*" Could there possibly be a Rabbid right here in the office of the SGAII-RD? While Glyker was in charge?

He closed the closet door and hurried down the hallway to investigate.

Unfortunately, he left the key card in the slot. . . .

CHAPTER 5:

Office Invasion

The three Rabbids strolled through the office, looking for the big, black, bushy fake mustache so they could play with it again. They talked to each other as they made their way down the hallways and through the offices. "Bwah bwah bwah BWAH bwah bwah!"

Whenever they saw a light switch, they flipped it. When they saw a button, they pressed it. Lights flicked on and off. Copy machines whirred awake, then shut back down.

They had just wandered into the office of an agent who had quit a week ago (muttering, "I never want to hear the word 'Rabbid' again!") when Glyker headed their way down the hall. One of them saw a light switch and flipped it.

The lights went off, and they stood in the office, their big eyes shining in the dark. On a computer, colored bubbles bounced around the screen. The Rabbids watched the bubbles, fascinated.

Out in the hallway Glyker rushed by. He didn't notice the Rabbids in the dark office.

Soon the Rabbids grew bored with the colored bubbles and moved on down the hall in the direction Glyker had come from.

As they passed the Closet of Super-Secret Experimental Spy Gadgets, the last Rabbid noticed the key card in the slot. He pushed it. *Click!*

The closet door slid open.

The three Rabbids stopped in their
tracks. "Bwoooooooh!" they crooned.
When they saw the interesting objects
in the closet, they forgot all about the
mustache they'd been looking for. (To
tell the truth, they'd forgotten about the
mustache approximately forty-two seconds
after they entered the office.)

The first Rabbid, who considered himself the leader, said, "Bwah bwah bwah bwah bwah bwah!" while pointing to his chest. He seemed to be claiming first dibs on the shiny gadgets. The other two Rabbids were too busy staring to care what he did.

The first Rabbid carefully considered the gadgets, trying to decide which one to take. Or maybe he'd take *more* than one. . . .

"Where *are* they?" Glyker asked himself. He'd searched the whole office without finding a single Rabbid. But he was sure he'd heard them.

And now, very faintly, in a different part of the office, he thought he heard another "bwah."

Could it be . . . back by the Closet of Super-Secret Experimental Spy Gadgets?

It'd better not be!

He ran back to the closet as fast as he could. When he got near it, he saw no Rabbids. But he did see something very bad.

The door was wide open.

Glyker was sure he'd closed the door. He slowed down, almost afraid to look in the closet. But when he did, it was clear that some highly experimental spy gadgets were . . . *missing*! Doing a quick scan of the closet, Glyker noted three empty spots on the wall.

He panicked and ran back down the hall, not even sure where he was going. The thought of three dangerous weapons in the hands of the Rabbids was absolutely appalling.

But actually, if Glyker had taken the time to look a little more carefully, he would have seen that there were *four* empty spots in the closet. . . .

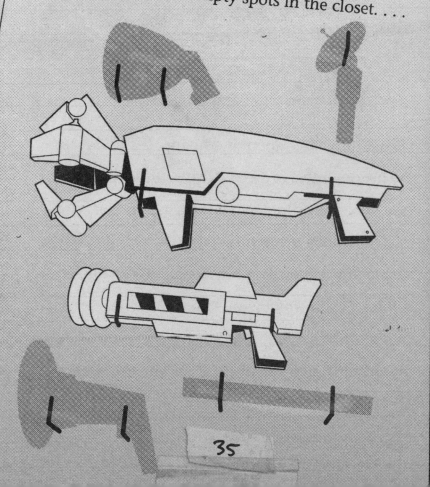

CHAPTER 6:
Very Attractive

Outside, the three Rabbids were hurrying away from the headquarters of the SGAII-RD, thrilled with their new toys. They couldn't wait to try them out!

The leader announced that he would be the first to try one of the shiny objects. "Bwah bwah bwoh bweeh bway bwah!" he said.

He was carrying two spy gadgets. He picked the shinier one and set the other one aside. He felt pretty sure this gleaming object did something, but

what? And how did you make it do the thing it did?

He tried listening to it. Sniffing it. Licking it. Rubbing it. Twirling it. Yelling at it. "BWAH BWAH BWAH!"

Finally, he found a button and pushed it.

Whoosh! Clank! An empty soda can flew through the air and stuck to the glittering metal baton. "BWAH HA!" cried the Rabbid, delighted.

He pushed the button again, and the can fell off the baton. "Bwaaaah," the Rabbid said, fascinated.

Next the Rabbid pointed the gadget at one of his fellow Rabbids, expecting it to make him fly through the air and stick to the baton like the soda can had. He pressed the button . . . and nothing happened. Confused, the Rabbid looked at the end of the baton. "BWAH BWAH BWAH!" he yelled at it, and pointed it at his fellow Rabbid again and pushed the button. Nothing happened. The other two Rabbids thought this was hilarious. They pointed and laughed, which made the Rabbid with the baton really mad.

The Rabbids didn't know it, but the experimental gadget was a powerful magnet. *Extremely* powerful. So powerful it could attract *any* kind of metal. Rabbids, of course, are not made of metal. But good luck trying to explain that to a Rabbid!

The Rabbid with the gadget spotted a kid drinking a soda. He held up the gadget and pushed the button, pointing it at the kid. *Whoosh!* The can flew out of the kid's hands! *Clank!* The can stuck to the baton. Soda sprayed all over the Rabbid holding the baton.

"BWAH HA HA HA!" laughed the other two Rabbids, pointing at the Rabbid with the gadget once again. It was even funnier now that he was soaked in sticky soda.

The Rabbid clicked the button on the baton again. The can fell off. It's impossible to know if he had started to figure out that the gadget only worked on metal. Probably not.

But for whatever reason, the Rabbid then decided to try moving on to bigger and better things than kids and cans of soda.

He pointed the baton at a moving car and clicked. . . .

The car swerved right toward the gadget, bumping up over the curb and onto the sidewalk! *SCREECH! BEEEEEP!* The driver frantically hit the brakes and blasted his horn, but he couldn't stop his car from zooming straight toward the Rabbid!

Click! At the last second the Rabbid hit the

button, turning off the magnet. The car stopped inches from the powerful device.

"Bwah bwah bwah bwah!" the Rabbid said happily. Soon the Rabbids were running around town, using the magnet to move cars, refrigerators, traffic signs, microwave ovens, bells, mailboxes, suits of armor, bank safes . . .

And very soon after that, calls started pouring into Glyker's office. . . .

CHAPTER 7:

Drop That Magnet!

The Rabbids were having a wonderful time with the Super-Magnet (even though they didn't know it was called that), using it to move huge metal objects all over town.

But one of the Rabbids hadn't gotten to hold the magnet yet. He thought it was his turn, so he grabbed the gadget out of another Rabbid's hands and ran with it. "BWAH!" yelled the Rabbid who'd been holding the magnet. He chased the Rabbid with the magnet, shouting "BWAH BWAH BWAH BWAH!" (Which probably meant "GIVE ME BACK THAT THING!")

As he ran, the Rabbid with the magnet looked around for something to use it on.

Then he spotted something perfect.

A big garbage truck was driving down the street. The Rabbid pointed the magnet at the truck and pushed the button. *Click!*

The truck swerved and started coming right at the Rabbid, moving faster and faster. The driver blasted his horn. *HONK! HONK! HONK!*

As the truck bore down on the Rabbid, he just stared at it, fascinated. He forgot he was supposed to click the magnet off before the truck reached the gadget.

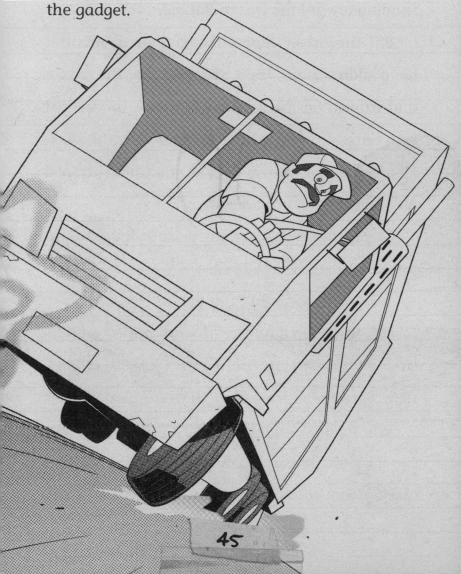

wing tips from furious callers, Agent Glyker arrived just in time to see the garbage truck zooming right at the Rabbid. "STOP!" he yelled, running toward the frozen Rabbid.

But the driver had already figured out that he couldn't stop. He'd stomped on the brake and yanked on the emergency brake, but he just kept barreling toward the invader with the stick. Finally, he opened the door of the truck, jumped out, and hit the ground rolling.

Seeing the huge garbage truck heading straight toward him, the Rabbid yelled "BWAH!" and threw the magnetic baton high in the air.

The truck lifted off the ground, tipped onto its side, and landed on the baton. *CRASH!* Garbage flew everywhere! Including all over Agent Glyker!

Wiping a banana peel off his face, Glyker saw the three Rabbids running away, but he couldn't chase them because he knew he had to recover the experimental gadget. After he made sure the driver was okay, Glyker started picking through the piles of stinking garbage to find the missing Super-Magnet. . . .

47

CHAPTER 8:

We See You!

In a nearby neighborhood, on a nice street with big houses and leafy trees, the three Rabbids pointed and laughed. "BWAH HA HA HA HA HA!"

What were they laughing at?

In one of the houses a man was taking a bath. He rinsed the soap off his face, looked for a towel, and was very surprised by what he saw.

He could see the street outside! The trees! The bushes! The parked cars! And he wasn't looking

through a window. He was looking right through the wall of his bathroom!

Something had turned the walls of his house transparent! He could see right through them!

And judging from the three Rabbids out on the sidewalk, pointing at him and laughing, everyone outside could see right through his walls too!

Stunned, the man reached for a towel. But in his rush to cover himself, he slipped and fell. Naked.

The Rabbids laughed even harder. "BWAH HA HA HA HA!"

How had the man's walls become completely see-through?

The Rabbids had used a very special gadget on his house: a Transparentizer. All they had to do was point the Transparentizer at a building and pull the trigger. Then they'd be able to see right through the walls! (Which is very useful for a secret spy investigating intruders.)

Once they realized what the device did, the Rabbids ran all over the city aiming it at walls and pulling the trigger. *Zworp!* Walls turned invisible, and everyone could see inside the buildings!

This was especially embarrassing for people inside bathrooms and dressing rooms. But to the Rabbids, it was hilarious.

People spotted the Rabbids zapping buildings with the weird-looking gadget just before the buildings' walls turned clear. Outraged citizens concluded that the Rabbids were behind all the see-through buildings! They immediately alerted the SGAII-RD, and the calls went straight to Agent Glyker's cell phone.

He was smelly from picking through garbage, but he'd gotten the Super-Magnet back. Now he drove his beat-up old car as fast as it could go to the address where the Rabbids had last been seen.

There they were. Laughing. And pointing. And laughing some more.

They were standing in front of a gymnasium with a transparent wall. Everyone could see right into the men's and women's locker rooms. People were scrambling to cover themselves with whatever clothes they could grab. One guy who didn't see an invisible wall ran right into it. *SMACK!*

The Rabbids are trying to rob us of our dignity! Glyker thought. He jumped out of his car and tried to sneak over to the Rabbids.

The Rabbids were so busy pointing and laughing at how ridiculous the naked humans looked that they didn't notice Glyker scurrying from tree to tree.

But he quickly ran out of trees.

He decided to go for broke. He leaped out from behind a tree and sprinted toward the three Rabbids. He remembered not to yell something like, "Stop in the name of the SGAII-RD!" Yelling tended to ruin the surprise.

They noticed him anyway. As he got closer, the Rabbid holding the Transparentizer aimed the device right at Glyker and pulled the trigger. *Zworp!*

He didn't know it worked on clothes, too. . . .

CHAPTER 9:

Naked Agent

Agent Glyker still had his clothes on, so technically he wasn't naked.

Technically.

But when everyone can see right through your clothes, it really doesn't matter whether you've got them on or not.

The Rabbids thought this was one of the funni-est things they'd ever seen. "BWAH HA HA HA!" they laughed, rolling on the ground and holding their sides.

Agent Glyker was devoted to his job. Even if everyone could see right through his clothes, he wasn't going to let an opportunity to catch a Rabbid pass him by. Especially a Rabbid who was laughing at him.

He kept on running toward the Rabbids. One of the laughing Rabbids noticed this. He stopped laughing and punched the Rabbid with the Transparentizer in the arm so he'd notice too.

That Rabbid got an idea.

He threw the Transparentizer as far as he could in one direction and started running as fast as he could in the other direction. His two fellow Rabbids ran with him.

Agent Glyker had to make a choice. Did he

keep chasing the Rabbids, or did he retrieve the Transparentizer?

He sighed. He couldn't let a Super-Secret Experimental Spy Gadget fall into the wrong hands. He had to go get it.

As he bent over to pick up the Transparentizer, he heard a voice say, "Okay, buddy—hold it right there." He turned around and saw a policeman. "What's the big idea, pal?" the policeman asked. "Forget to get dressed this morning?"

One of the Rabbids thought it was time to try out the device *he'd* taken from the Closet of Super-Secret Experimental Spy Gadgets. He kept pointing it at buildings and people and pressing buttons, but nothing happened.

As the Rabbids wandered through a park, the Rabbid holding the gadget grew more and more frustrated with his device. Why wouldn't it *do* something? He started yelling at it, putting his mouth close to the object. "BWAH BWAH BWAH BWIGH BWOH BWAH!"

One of the other Rabbids noticed something. A woman was sitting on a park bench frowning at her phone. Out of the phone came the voice of the yelling Rabbid: "BWAH BWAH BWAH BWIGH BWOH BWAH!"

It didn't take long for the Rabbids to figure out

what the gadget did: it let you talk through other people's phones! The Rabbids ran all over the city looking for people talking on their phones. (They weren't hard to find.) Then they took turns yelling into the gadget and laughing at the startled reactions of the people holding the phones.

One woman on a bench kept trying to make calls on her phone, but all she heard was "BWAH BWAH BWAH!" She turned to the old lady next to her and said, "Someone has taken over our phones! HOW CAN WE SURVIVE WITHOUT OUR PHONES?!"

The old lady nodded and said, "That's nice, dear."

CHAPTER 10:

Whack-a-Spy

Agent Glyker had recovered the Super-Magnet and the Transparentizer, and he had changed his outfit back to normal so it was no longer transparent. He figured he only had one more gadget to retrieve from the Rabbids. All he had to do was wait for a call to come in. He sat in his beat-up old car at a spot right in the center of the city, waiting. He hoped it came soon. It had been a long, hard day so far. He'd had a terrible time explaining himself to the police officer, and now he had a citation for indecent exposure to deal with. He hoped Uncle Jim wouldn't mind paying the fee, since it was a work-related expense.

His cell phone rang.

"Agent Glyker, Temporary Director-in-Charge," he said. "Do you have a Rabbid–related emergency?"

"Yes!" a man with a high-pitched voice squeaked. "The Rabbids are BWAH BWAH BWAH BWAH BWAH BWAH!"

Glyker looked confused. "Could you repeat that, please?"

"I said the Rabbids are BWAH BWAH BWAH BWAH BWAH BWAH! No one can BWAH BWAH BWAH!"

"I'm sorry, sir, but I can't understand what you're—"

"BWAH BWAH BWAH BWAH!"

The caller hung up. Glyker stared at his phone.

Had the man who called been taken hostage by the Rabbids? Were they yelling into his phone, demanding ransom money? How much money did "BWAH BWAH BWAH" equal?

Glyker couldn't just sit in his car waiting anymore. He turned his key in the ignition, threw the car into drive, and peeled out. He'd cruise around the city, hoping to spot the Rabbids before they took anyone else hostage!

Of course, the Rabbids hadn't taken any *people*

hostage. But they had taken the city's phone system hostage. Every time someone tried to make a phone call, all anyone heard was "BWAH BWAH BWAH!"

That meant nobody could call their doctor, or the police, or the fire department. No one could do any business on the phone. No teenagers could call their parents and ask them to pick them up. No one could order any pizzas. Without phones, the city was paralyzed.

Glyker got lucky. He spotted the Rabbids downtown, where there were lots of people trying to talk on their phones. "BWAH BWAH BWAH HA HA HA!" could be heard coming from every single phone.

One of the Rabbids was holding the experimental gadget, gleefully talking into it: "BWAH BWAH BWOH BWOO BWAY BWAY BWEE BWAH BWAH!" The other two Rabbids were pointing at frustrated people with phones and laughing at them.

The Rabbid was so focused on talking into the device that Glyker was confident he could sneak up on him this time.

Using all his spy training, Agent Glyker stealthily crept toward the Rabbid with the device. At the last second, he pounced!

"BWAH!" yelled the startled Rabbid.

Glyker tried to pick up the Rabbid and carry
him to his car, but the Rabbid started whacking him with the Telephone Disrupter. *WHACK!*
WHACK! WHACK!

"Ouch!" Glyker yelled. "Stop that! I'm not
going to hurt you!"

But the Rabbid kept on whacking the agent. The Rabbid was actually having fun. "BWAH HA HA HA!" he laughed, banging Glyker on the head over and over.

Glyker had to use both hands to grab the gadget. But that meant he wasn't holding on to the Rabbid anymore. The minute he let go, the Rabbid ran off with his two fellow invaders.

At least Glyker had the third gadget back. (Plus a headache.) He may not have captured a Rabbid, but he'd succeeded in recovering all the experimental spy gadgets.

Or so he thought. . . .

CHAPTER 11:

You Big Baby

If you're better at noticing things than poor Agent Glyker is, you'll remember that when the Rabbids visited the Closet of Super-Secret Experimental Spy Gadgets, they left four spots empty.

Not three. Four.

That meant they still had one Super-Secret Experimental Spy Gadget left. And they were eager to find out just what it could do.

From their experience with the first three devices,

the Rabbids had learned to point the gadgets at people or things and press a button or pull a trigger.

But what should they point it at?

Suddenly they heard a loud, annoying sound. "WAAAAH!" It was a baby crying. "WAAAAAAH!" the baby screamed.

Two of the Rabbids covered their ears. The third Rabbid pointed the last experimental gadget at the baby. *Click!*

Glyker parked his car in Director Stern's parking place—the nice shady spot closest to the door. He gathered the three experimental objects in his arms and started to go inside. Maybe he'd take a nice nap on Director Stern's couch. . . .

BOOM. The earth shook. BOOM. BOOM. BOOM.

What was that low rumbling? Why was the ground trembling? Was it an earthquake? A thunderstorm? A tsunami?

No. It was a baby. "GOO GOO!"

When Agent Glyker heard the loud "Goo goo," he looked around, but saw nothing.

Then he looked up.

A huge baby was stomping through the city! Its curly hair reached into the clouds! Its diaper was the size of a blimp! Its drool hit the ground and formed instant ponds! SPLAT!

"That's a big baby," Glyker said to himself, astonished by the tremendous infant.

71

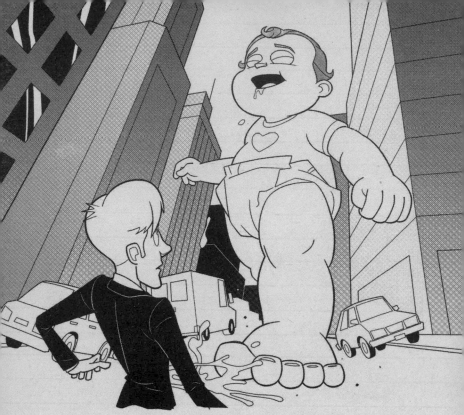

"How did this happen?" Glyker wondered for about two seconds. Then he remembered rumors around the SGAII-RD about a Super-Extra-Secret Highly Experimental Gadget that made things grow to an enormous size. He'd heard the name "the Biggifier" whispered in awe.

The Rabbids had biggified a baby. Glyker was sure of it.

But right now, it didn't really matter how it had happened. There was a giant baby to deal with. Glyker needed to get the Biggifier back from the Rabbids, use it to shrink the baby (he was hoping the Biggifier had some kind of reverse, littlizing feature), and return the baby to its parents.

He tossed the three gadgets back in his car, jumped in, and drove off in the direction of the baby. The baby was so big that it was very easy to keep track of.

Agent Glyker figured that he'd find the Rabbids near the baby. Based on all the pointing and laughing he'd seen them do, he guessed they'd be excited about the baby they'd biggified.

He was right.

The Rabbids were running to keep up with the giant baby, laughing and cheering every time it knocked over a statue or crushed an empty car. This was the most fun thing they'd done with one of the gadgets yet!

"GOO GOO GAH GAH!" thundered the huge baby.
"BWAH HA HA HA!" laughed the Rabbids.

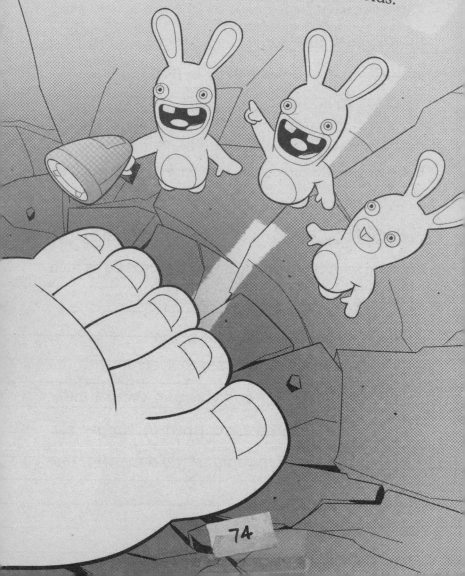

Glyker pulled up in his crummy brown car and screeched to a halt. He'd driven as close to the Rabbids as he could get.

One of them was carrying the Biggifier.

Glyker wasted no time. He ran at the Rabbid with the gadget, reaching out to grab it.

The Rabbid saw him coming, whipped around, aimed the Biggifier, and fired! *Zhwaarpp!*

CHAPTER 12:

Gigantic!

Agent Glyker grew. And grew. And GREW! Until he was no longer Agent Glyker. He was GIANT Glyker!

"Bwoooooh," the Rabbids said, looking up at the gigantic man.

"Well," thought Glyker. "This is handy."

Now that he was huge, it was simple for Glyker to take one or two steps and quickly reach the baby. He picked the baby up and carried it in his arms so it would stop crushing everything.

Next he reached down and took the Biggifier away from the Rabbid. Glyker was so big that if he wanted to take something, there was really nothing the Rabbid could do about it.

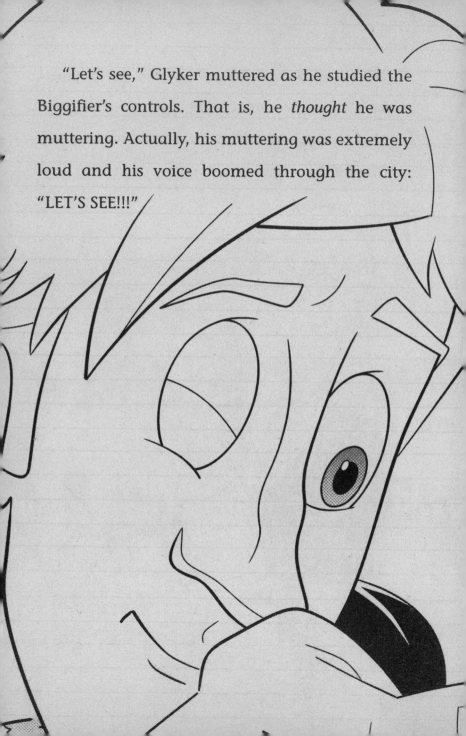

"Let's see," Glyker muttered as he studied the Biggifier's controls. That is, he *thought* he was muttering. Actually, his muttering was extremely loud and his voice boomed through the city: "LET'S SEE!!!"

The Biggifier was like a tiny stick in Glyker's huge hands, but he managed to find a switch that he thought might reverse the growing effect. By using just the corner of his smallest fingernail, he flipped the switch.

"HERE GOES NOTHING," he said in his tremendous voice as he set the baby down and aimed the gadget at her (it was a girl—a big, big girl). *Ppraawhz!*

It worked! The baby girl shrank down to her normal size. Her grateful parents scooped her up in their arms and hurried home, hoping they wouldn't get in trouble for all the damage she'd done. It wasn't their fault she'd become freakishly huge.

Giant Glyker looked down at the ground, hoping to spot the Rabbids and scoop them up in his enormous hands. But he didn't see the Rabbids anywhere.

Then, out of the corner of his giant eye, he saw something yellow moving in the sky. A Rabbid spaceship!

Glyker leaped high into the air, trying to catch the spaceship, but it buzzed off into the stratosphere, far beyond his reach. As he watched them fly out of sight, Glyker thought his giant ears heard laughter: "BWAH HA HA HA HA!"

Sighing, Agent Glyker aimed the reversed Biggifier at himself and pushed the button. *Ppraawhz!*

CHAPTER 13:

No Longer Large and in Charge

Back to his normal size, Agent Glyker returned to the SGAII-RD building. He'd managed to recover all four missing experimental gadgets, but once again he'd failed to catch a Rabbid.

Just as he finished hanging the devices on their hooks, he heard Director Stern returning from his vacation. "Glyker?" his uncle called gently. "Are you here?"

Glyker closed the door, pulled out the key card,

and hurried down the hallway to his boss's office.
He hoped he hadn't pushed anything on the desk
out of place when he put his feet up on it. Or left
any shoe prints.

"Welcome back, Uncle Jim!" Glyker greeted Director Stern cheerfully. His uncle was in such a good mood from his vacation that he didn't even object to his nephew calling him "Uncle Jim" in the office. "How was your vacation?"

"Excellent!" Director Stern said, settling into his big leather desk chair. "Very relaxing. I got away from phones, e-mail, the Internet, TV, radio, and newspapers, so I heard absolutely nothing about those pesky Rabbids. You didn't happen to catch one, did you?"

DIRECTOR
STERN

"No, I'm afraid not," Glyker admitted.

Stern chuckled. "Well, they're pretty slippery.
We'll get one eventually."

Glyker couldn't believe how much good Stern's
vacation had done him. It was as though his uncle
were a completely different—much nicer—person.

"So," Stern asked. "How'd everything go while
I was gone? Any problems?"

"Everything went great!" Glyker lied. "No problems at all!" He had assumed that Director Stern would have heard on the news all about what had happened, or read about it online, but since he hadn't, why bring it up now? This meant that Glyker would have to pay his citation for indecent exposure himself . . . but he did have some of his birthday money left over.

"Wonderful!" Stern said. "Well, if you'll excuse me, I picked up the latest edition of the newspaper on my way in here, so I think I'll just spend a few minutes catching up on what's been happening."

Glyker turned pale. "R-right," he stammered. "I'll, um, be in my office."

He hurried out of Stern's office. The director opened his folded newspaper and looked at the headline for the first time: RABBID RAMPAGE!!

Glyker had almost slipped out the exit, when he heard his uncle bellow, "GLYKER!!!"

Attention !!!

Glyker's To-Do List:

1. File expense report to be reimbursed for robot parts.

2. Download heavy metal albums and study lyrics for clues about Rabbid motives.

3. Find out what kind of cake Uncle Jim likes best.

4. Ask Mom to bake a cake for Uncle Jim.

5. Find out who infiltrated my online dating profile and replaced my personal photo with a picture of a toilet.

bulbous eyes